Titus the Magnificent

The Adventures of Titus

Written by Lucille M. Johnson

Illustrated by Angie Derrick

Inspiring Voices books may be ordered through booksellers or by contacting:

Inspiring Voices
1663 Liberty Drive
Bloomington, IN 47403
www.inspiringvoices.com
1 (866) 697-5313

ISBN: 978-1-4624-0755-2 (sc)
ISBN: 978-1-4624-0754-5 (e)

Printed in the United States of America.

Inspiring Voices rev. date: 9/26/2013

Dedication

I dedicate this in loving memory of my daughter Donna Marie.
And to all my friends who have supported me on this
writing journey, my heartfelt thanks.

Table of Contents

If I Could Talk

If I could talk, I would have a lot to say. I'm pretty sharp, if I don't say so myself. Some people might say that I'm a bit prideful. I don't give that much thought because I have a lot of sterling qualities. To cite one such quality, I really love people! There's a problem with that, though. I'm a big dog, and I tend to knock some people off of their feet.

My owner, Patti, had an accident on her bike recently. Don't ask me any questions about it because it's too involved for me to explain. She had surgery on her knee and we can't go out to play together right now. So my other owners—John, Rachel and Levi—take me out for walks instead. I miss Patti, though, so I'm a little sad, and I know she is, too.

Well, enough conversation—I've got to get to sleep. So much to do, and so little time to do it all!

Much love,
Titus, the Exceedingly Talented Dog

WELCOME TO NY TITUS!!

Happy New Year

I aim to be the first dog ever to be on the platform in New York City's Time Square with many news reporters to lead in the countdown to the New Year. I received a special invitation from the mayor of New York City. It was engraved, of course. Nothing less would do.

I'm to represent all of the dogs of America to herald in the New Year. I'm not surprised by this invitation to the Big Apple, because my fame has spread far and wide.

Little did John and Patti realize when they brought me home, what a treasure they had in their hands. Well, I can't go on and on about that right now.

It is my understanding that the crowds are incredibly large—massive, is more like it—and when I return, I expect a brass band to meet me at the airport. You can dispense with the confetti and ticker-tape parade and just bring the mayor and other dignitaries.

So long for now, and Happy New Year!

The talented and amazing,
Titus the Magnificent

DON'T SIT,
GET FIT!
NO PAIN
GAIN

Slim and Trim at the Gym

Here we are, another year ahead of us, and I intend to make good use of it. It is so exciting to see what adventures await me. I am not a slacker, by any means. I'm a dog of ACTION.

All of my plans for the New Year are swirling around in my head. I do want to start the year out right, so I'm going to head down to the gym and take out membership for the year. Slim and trim, that's me! I need to keep up appearances so that the other dogs will have a role model to follow: Titus the most fit dog in the area.

I'm a self-starter and I really don't need a trainer. As a matter of fact, in a few months, I'll be so buff that I can start training other dogs. What a great idea! Lightbulbs are going off in my brain all the time. I'll take a bone to chew on and head out the door. Fitness Center, here I come!

Titus the Fittest,
That's me

A Special Valentine's Day

There's someone I'm interested in. Now no one knows about her but me. She is really cute and lives in Seattle. Quite a distance from Renton, but to get to see her is worth the trip. I just bought a custom made motorcycle and it gets me where I want to go in a hurry. I'll give her a call and invite her out for Valentine's day. I can see us now on that motorcycle.

I'm making reservations at The Space Needle. Nothing but the best for my gal. I'm ordering a bouquet of red roses for her. Her name is Rosemarie and she really likes me. I think I have everything under control. What an evening it will be. We will be the best-looking couple in Seattle.

The most romantic dog,
Titus

CORNS
CARRO
TOMATOES
PEAS

A Spring in My Step

What's that I see down in the ground? It's a flower—a crocus! Now that gives me an idea for this summer—a veggie garden for my family. Won't that please them? I'll start planning now. I'm a great digger and in no time, I'll have that garden growing.

There is really no end to my talent. A farmer—that's me! A little research and I'm digging up the ground. Of course, it will need watering. Now, how will I do that? Oh, I just had a magnificent thought! I'll hire a plane to fly over and pour water over my spectacular garden. Hoorah for me!

If anyone has any helpful suggestions, just e-mail me and I'll take all suggestions into consideration. I'm not saying I'll use any of your ideas, just think about them. After all, who has the most incredible brain of all dogs? It's me, of course.

Farmer of the Year,
Titus

A Very Special Easter

I have a great idea for this Easter. I just received an e-mail that a family in our town are having some difficult times. What I will do is to start a fund raiser for them so that they can have a wonderful Easter. It feels so good to give.

We are planning a big Easter egg hunt, with many children coming to look for eggs. What fun! Easter morning I'm joining the family for church. Maybe I'll ask John if I can drive the car. I just got my driver's license, so off we will go if he says yes.

The Great Easter Planner,
Titus

Mother's Day

It's me, Titus the Superdog, proclaiming that spring is here, and there's a spring in my step! There are a lot of changes going on, and I'm trying to adjust to all of them. It is so overwhelming just observing all of the change!

Walking along, I see some new tulips. They are just beautiful! Mother's Day is fast approaching and wouldn't a bouquet of tulips just bring a smile to Patti's face? One problem though—they are not on our property. If I pick them for Patti, that's stealing. I'm really wondering what I should do... After careful consideration, I decide not to pick them. I am such a good dog!

It's the thought that counts and Patti would be so delighted with me, that I made the right decision. Happy Mother's Day, Patti!

As ever,
Titus, the Most Obedient Dog

DAD

Father's Day

With Father's Day fast approaching, I think that it would be a great gesture on my part to do all I can for John, who works so hard to make sure I have enough dog biscuits, toys to play with, and visits to the vet. Sometimes there are lots of visits to the vet, which is not my favorite place!

Since I don't do very well shopping, due to all of the No Dogs Allowed rules, I can only repay him by being obedient. Not always easy... I sleep on the floor next to him, give him many licks, and entertain him in the best way that I can. I wag my tail and will bark very loudly!

Happy Father's Day!

Your Super Smart Dog,
Titus

Dog Days of Summer

Calling all dogs! The pool is now open in my yard. There's an expression—not one that I particularly care about—called "Dog Days of Summer," referring to the very hot, sizzling summer days.

Now I know how exhausting the heat can be, so out of the goodness of my heart, I'm offering FREE days of fun-filled splashing in my pool. Come one, come all weary dogs! There will be refreshments, and you'll be glad you did! There will be a possibility of some light snacks, such as Bar-B-Q "hot dogs" (no pun intended).

Most humbly,
Titus the Magnificent Host

Rocky

Word has come to me that there is a dog in our vicinity who eats small stones. You might be gasping in disbelief, but it's true. Naturally, this has upset his digestive system.

I may be away from home for a little bit to pay Rocky a visit. I've been in touch with Dr. Bark and he informs me that he is unable to help him. I'm putting some dog biscuits in my backpack to tide me over while I'm away. Needless to say, I can't stay away very long as then there would be nobody to take care of John and Patti.

By the way, due to my incredible humility, I've neglected to mention that I've counseled many dogs and they have profited from my expert, outstanding advice. I'm certain that when I meet with Rocky, he will be totally cured from eating small stones.

Most humbly,
Titus the Brilliant Counselor

The Great Turkey Hunt

Thanksgiving is fast approaching and I want to give my family the very best Thanksgiving gift I can. Naturally, my mind is spinning with ideas. Then it hit me! A wild turkey! What an inspiration, what a wonderful gift. Our house is kind of out in the country, and I know there has to be a wild turkey out there somewhere. Magnificent thought!

I must gather up what is necessary for this turkey hunt. I'll call some of my dog buddies from the neighboring town. The more, the merrier. I'll send out invitations through a pigeon carrier. Another sweet idea!

Now, how to catch the turkey... Of course, I'll use a net. All of us dogs will dig a hole and cover it with leaves, and then down goes the turkey, and we pull it out with the net. Won't John and Patti be so proud of me and my remarkable ideas!

I could go on and on, but I won't. We caught that turkey and what a tasty meal it will make. Maybe my doggy companions can stay for Thanksgiving dinner. What a lovely Thanksgiving it will be, all due to my great thinking capacity!

Ever and always,
Titus the Hunter

In Search of the Perfect Christmas Tree

I'm packing all of my bones and, of course, I have to pack quite a few. I'm on my way to Alaska and plan to bring back the best Christmas tree from there.

Can't you just see the happy faces of my family when I return with this outstanding tree? I'm getting ahead of myself though, because I'm so excited. I have three suitcases packed full of bones. I hope it doesn't cost a lot to check them in to the airline. I'm flying first-class. Now, get this, I've been invited to join the pilots as they fly one of the best planes, the Boeing 787, to Alaska. You may be wondering why they invited me. Well, to answer your question, they need my help to fly the plane.

When I arrive, they will have a sled and a team of Husky dogs to get me to my destination—the Forest of Christmas Trees. I will give instructions to those Huskies on how to run as swiftly as possible. I will be seated on the sled, right up front, barking out orders. It will be an amazing trip and, of course, it will all be accomplished with my outstanding leadership.

Merry Christmas!
Titus, the Leader of the Pack

Special Thanks

With heartfelt thanks to:

Angie Derrick—Thank you for gracing my book with your beautiful illustrations. They will bring delight to so many children.

Jackie Donnelly—I am so grateful for your guidance and all your hard work in helping me with this manuscript.

CPSIA information can be obtained
at www.ICGtesting.com
Printed in the USA
LVIC06n2053101013
356235LV00002B